SUPER
OPTICAL
ILLUSIONS

SUPER OPTICAL ILLUSIONS

GIANNI A. SARCONE
AND MARIE-JO WAEBER

CHAPTER 1

ALL ABOUT COLOURS

When we see a colour, we really see light being reflected from an object, which our brain "reads" as a particular colour. There's no colour in nature, because colours are actually all created in your brain!

Sometimes, as you'll see in the following pages, your brain can be tricked and confuses colours and shade

DO YOU SEE SOME GREEN DOTS?

Actually, they're not green but black! You see green because of the colour of the background and the neighbouring shaded dots. Incredible, isn't it?

This football is covered with pentagonal and hexagonal panels.

Are panels A and B exactly the same SHADE?

Yes, they are! They look like different shades because they are surrounded by lighter and darker panels. Your brain is tricked by the contrast!

After approximately 20 seconds, the colours of the cat's face gradually disappear. Nothing is left behind but its grin!

To create the illusion of balance ...
stare at the fly in the right hand picture for 30 seconds, then look at the cow again. The photograph will look normal!

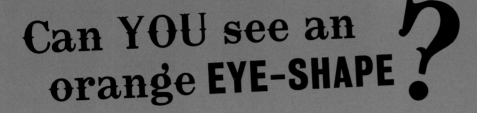

Can YOU see an orange EYE-SHAPE?

The dark orange glow of the outline is created by black lines on the yellow background. If you look closely you will see that there actually isn't any orange in this picture at all!

If you really concentrate on the middle of the picture, you might even get the eye to vanish!

Take a good look at this Greek painting. Are the arch shapes in the bottom and top row all the same **colour** and **shade**?

They are! This is hard to see because the human eye sees the outline of an object in relation to the colour of its background. Because the backgrounds are different colours it looks like the arches are, as well!

It looks like this cat has two green eyes, but really only one eye is green.

HOW DOES THAT WORK ?!

The right eye is grey, but seems tinted green because of the purple colour around it. When you look at the grey eye, your brain subtracts a bit of purple from the cat's face, which makes the eye look green. Cool, huh?

The colours of the rainbow in **figure A** are faded. To make them look stronger, stare at the white dot in **figure B** for 20 to 30 seconds, then shift your gaze back to **figure A**.

AMAZING, isn't it?

11

MATCH a pair of blue squares that have the same HUE and BRIGHTNESS.

Is it **A** and **C**, or **A** and **D**, or **B** and **C**, or maybe **B** and **D**?

A

B

C

D

Answer: A is exactly the same shade as D, although the different backgrounds make A appear brighter than D.

Concentrate only on the square panels of the cubes

(the real one and its reflection).

WHICH PANELS SEEM DARKER ?

In reality, the square panels of both cubes are identical! The illusion is created by the contrast between the backgrounds - in particular their brightness.

?

Then decide which ones have **YELLOW** inner circles, and which ones have **BLUE** inner circles.

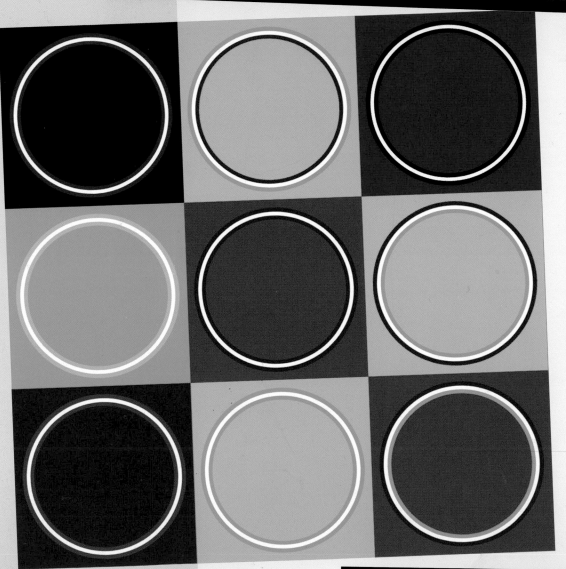

Ninety per cent of people answer that the rings in the first column have a blue inner circle, and those in the second and third columns have a yellow one. In fact, the middle colour inside all the rings is white!

CHAPTER 2

WOW... IT MOVES!

Some repeated patterns can look like they are in motion. This is caused by very fast movements of your eyes that happen without you controlling them.

Be careful not to **stare** at this one for too long or you might become hypnotized!

Can you see the reddish portion of the pattern pulsating or throbbing? Try staring at it for a while and matching the "pulsations" of the picture with the beat of your heart!

If you scan this picture quickly with your eyes, you may see the vertical pink and blue patterns **move** in changing directions!

The wavy, coloured lines seem to **wink** and **flicker** just like Christmas lights!

17

FEELING DIZZY YET?

LOOK at the blurred black heart for a while. Do you notice something strange ?

It appears to PULSATE and EXPAND!

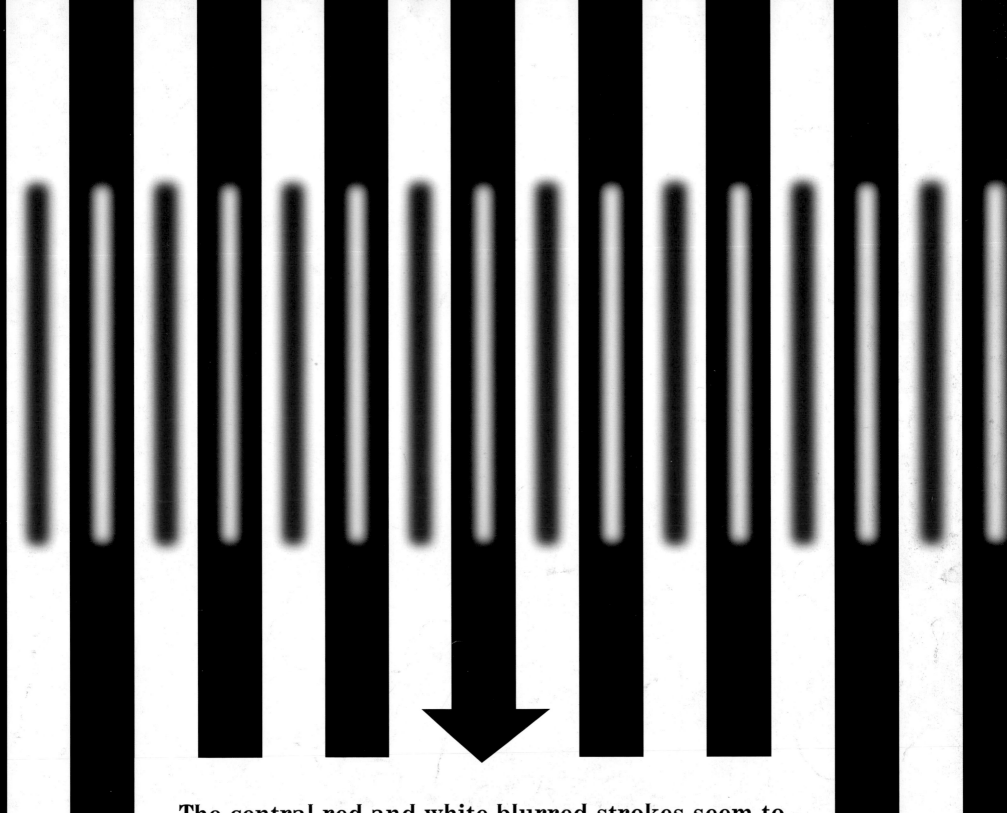

The central red and white blurred strokes seem to
move and to **SHRINK** or **EXPAND**.

19

Although this image is of course totally still, the **COFFEE BEANS** seem to **JUMP!**

Sometimes this illusion works better when you don't look directly at the coffee beans... for example when you are reading this text!

The three circular patterns will start to turn! Your brain is misreading the blurred dots as motion signals – and "thinks" they are actually moving.

Move your head **BACKWARDS** and **FORWARDS**, keeping your eyes fixed on the central cross in the image.

Shift your gaze around this pattern and dark dots will appear and disappear at the corners of the white squares.

CAN YOU TELL WHO

IS IN THIS PICTURE ?

It's **FRANK... ENSTEIN'S** monster! Look at the image from a distance to see him more clearly.

THIS CIRCULAR SHAPE IS A MANDALA.

It pulsates in tune with your brain waves! Repeating shapes and colour often trick the brain into seeing motion.

HOLD ON TIGHT!

The drops seem to move **UP** and **DOWN** and the straight yellow lines **WAVE** and **WOBBLE**!

Did you know? An **ILLUSION** of seeing movement triggers similar brain areas as **REAL** motion.

24

This bat seems to **FLUTTER, MOVE AND EXPAND.**

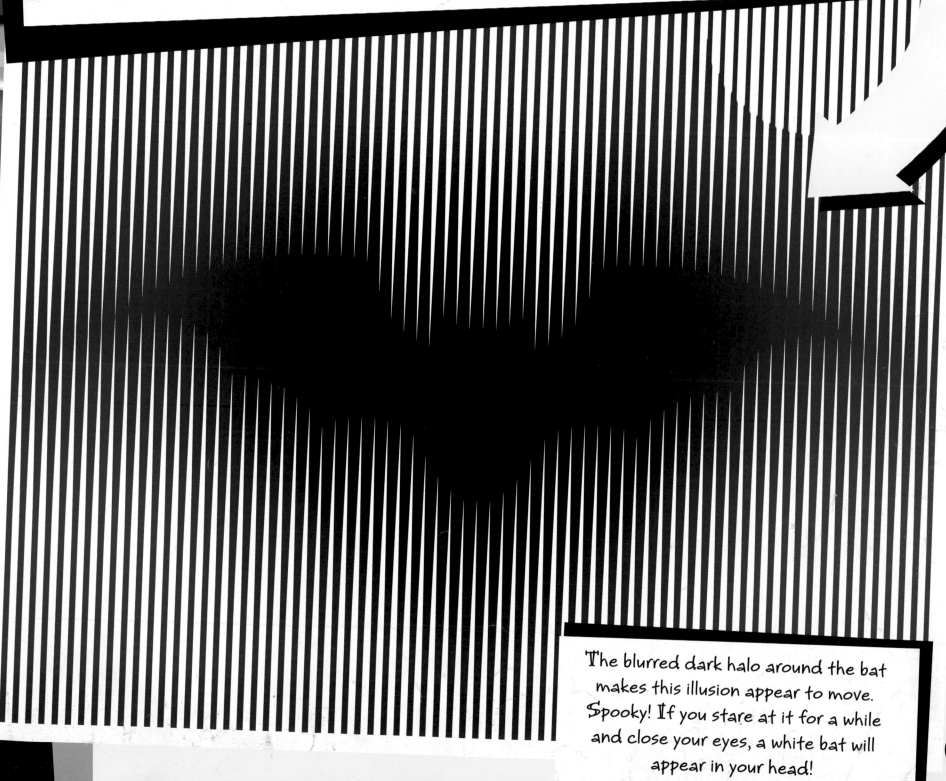

The blurred dark halo around the bat makes this illusion appear to move. Spooky! If you stare at it for a while and close your eyes, a white bat will appear in your head!

CHAPTER 3

IMPOSSIBLE PUZZLING & CAMOUFLAGED UNBELIEVABLE THINGS!

When the lines of a drawing are badly linked, the result can be an "impossible figure": a shape that looks normal at first, but cannot exist in reality.

Depending on the way you look at them, some pictures can also have two different meanings or even hide another picture.

IMPOSSIBLE AQUEDUCT

No builder could construct this!

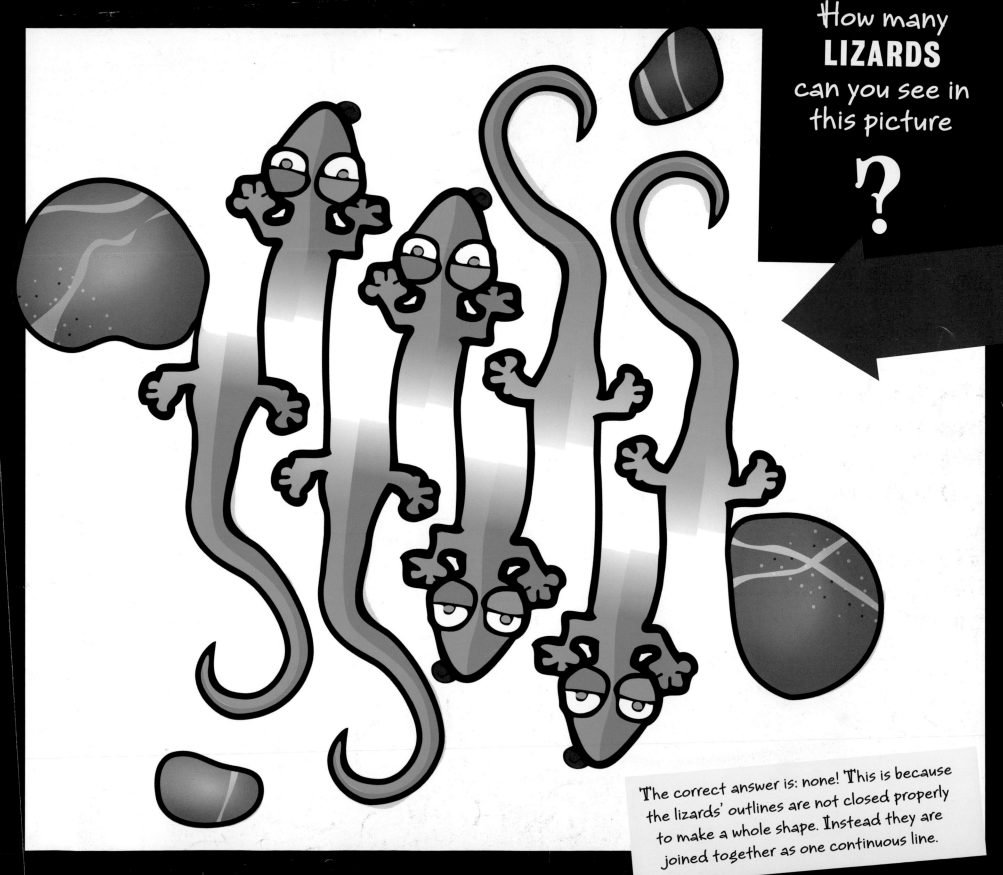

The correct answer is: none! This is because the lizards' outlines are not closed properly to make a whole shape. Instead they are joined together as one continuous line.

CAN YOU SPOT

a COMPLETE FIGURE in this picture?

?

Didn't think so! The top and bottom half of each character aren't actually connected to make a full shape. In fact, each figure is reversed along an axis in the middle of the image, where the green and black shapes are swapped. Can you see where?

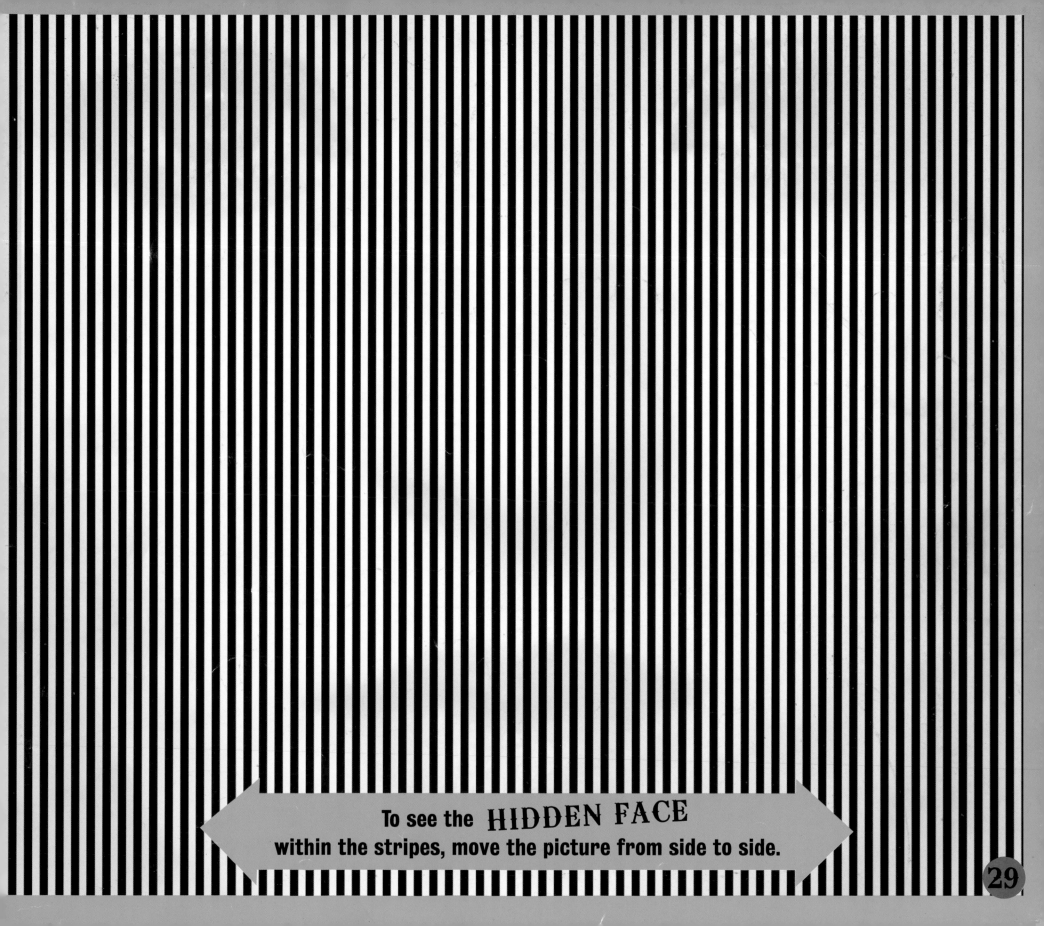

To see the HIDDEN FACE within the stripes, move the picture from side to side.

29

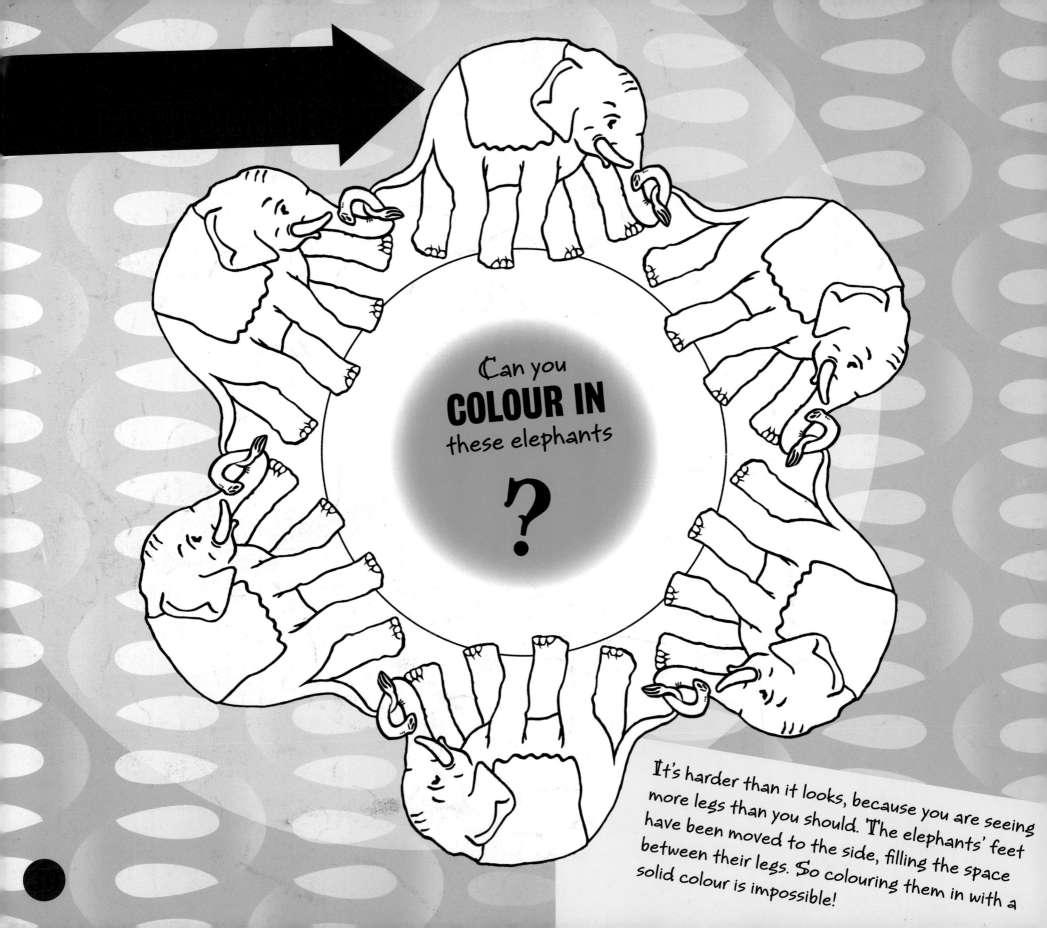

Can you **COLOUR IN** these elephants **?**

It's harder than it looks, because you are seeing more legs than you should. The elephants' feet have been moved to the side, filling the space between their legs. So colouring them in with a solid colour is impossible!

Does the window open **outwards** or **inwards**?

?

Is the front door of Lea's house **narrow** or **wide**?

There's no right answer to those questions, because this picture contains "impossible objects". The second marble column of the door blends with the empty space under the arch, and the window faces either to the right or to the left, depending on how you look at it.

If you **LOOK** at the **CENTRE** of this photograph for a while ...

a **SPOOKY FACE** will suddenly **APPEAR**!

(Its nose is the woman's shadow.)

This kind of illusion happens because humans have a tendency to see familiar shapes - even if they're not there.

A bar of chocolate is cut into six pieces and put back together to produce an extra piece of chocolate from nothing!

START

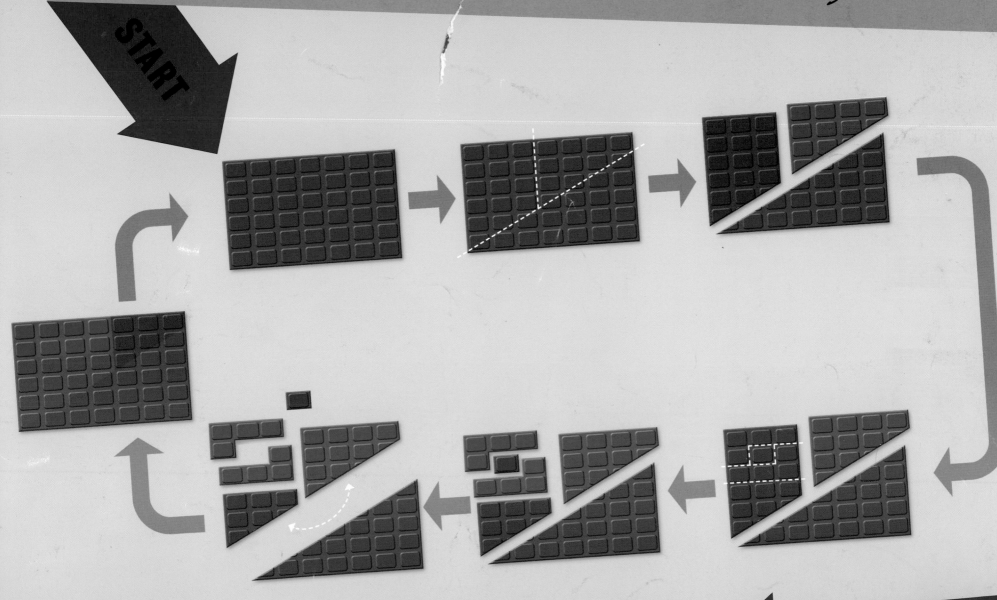

HOW IS THIS POSSIBLE ?

When a small piece of chocolate is removed from the bar and the remaining pieces ck together, they form a slightly shorter rectangle. The difference is too small ee with the naked eye so that the bar looks as if it is the same size as before.

First-time viewers do not usually see the four circles against th... backg... put ba... to s...

WHAT HAPPENS if the girl climbs up the stairs to the platform **?**

The answer is, not much! The platform and stairs form an impossible continuous loop. The girl could walk around in a circle forever and never get any higher!

CHAPTER 4

SIZE AND SHAPE CONFUSION. STRAIGHT or NOT?

The actual size of an object and the size it appears to be are two very different things. Shape confusion and errors in judging size have various causes, including the fact that we think in 3D, even when we look at 2D photos or drawings.

Which goldfish is **longer**?

Both are the same size. The bottom fish seems larger because it is surrounded by a smaller space.

Move your eyes up and down the picture ...

Are the thin, blue lines **straight** and **parallel** to each other?

Although they seem to move away from and get closer to each other, the lines are perfectly parallel! The pattern of leaves in the background creates the illusion that the blue lines are tilting.

This **SNAIL SHELL** looks like a **SPIRAL**, but the recurring pattern is actually made up of several circles!

If you don't believe it, use your finger to trace along the lines.

In these three atoms, the red cores are different sizes.

Which one is the LARGEST

AND

which one is the SMALLEST ?

1.

2.

3.

The red disc in figure 1 is the largest, while the disc in figure 3 is the smallest. It's hard to guess the real size of objects, because the perception of size is "relative". That means you judge the size of an object according to the objects around it.

WOW!

That's a neat sidekick! In this picture, the blue punching bag looks larger than the red one.

But are you SURE?

Use a ruler or trace the shape outlined with red dashes, and use it to check the size of the two punching bags. You'll see...

STRAIGHT OR NOT?

Is anything in the picture STRAIGHT?

The chequered frames are perfectly straight! The small black and white squares form wavy lines that interfere with how you see the straight lines, making the frames appear wonky.

Are these two book covers the SAME SIZE ?

Do the pictures and titles have exactly the SAME LENGTH and WIDTH?

Yes they do! The cover of the left book appears longer and narrower, but in reality the book covers are exactly the same size. This is the case for the words and illustrations too!

AROUND
AND
AROUND

Although the rings seem to spiral in towards each other, each one of them is perfectly round. What's more, if you concentrate on the picture's centre while moving your head backwards and forwards, the rings seem to turn.

43

Is the giraffe **TALLER** than the length of the dog ...

OR

is the dog **LONGER** than the height of the giraffe?

The height of the giraffe is exactly equal to the whole length of the dog. But most people think that the dog is longer.

If you connected the small white spots in the four **RED BALLS** together, would you get a perfect square? What about the spots in the **BLUE BALLS** ?

If you connect the white spots of the blue balls, you will outline a perfect square. You won't in the red.

Executive Editor – Selina Wood
Art Designers – Dani Lurie, Amy Clarke
Senior Editor – Anna Bowles

This is a Carlton book

Artworks and Text © Gianni A. Sarcone, Archimedes-lab.com

Design © Carlton Books Limited 2014

Published in 2017 by Carlton Books Limited,
An imprint of the Carlton Publishing Group,
20 Mortimer Street, London W1T 3JW

A catalogue record for this book is available from the British Library.

ISBN: 978-1-78312-252-3

Printed in Dongguan, China